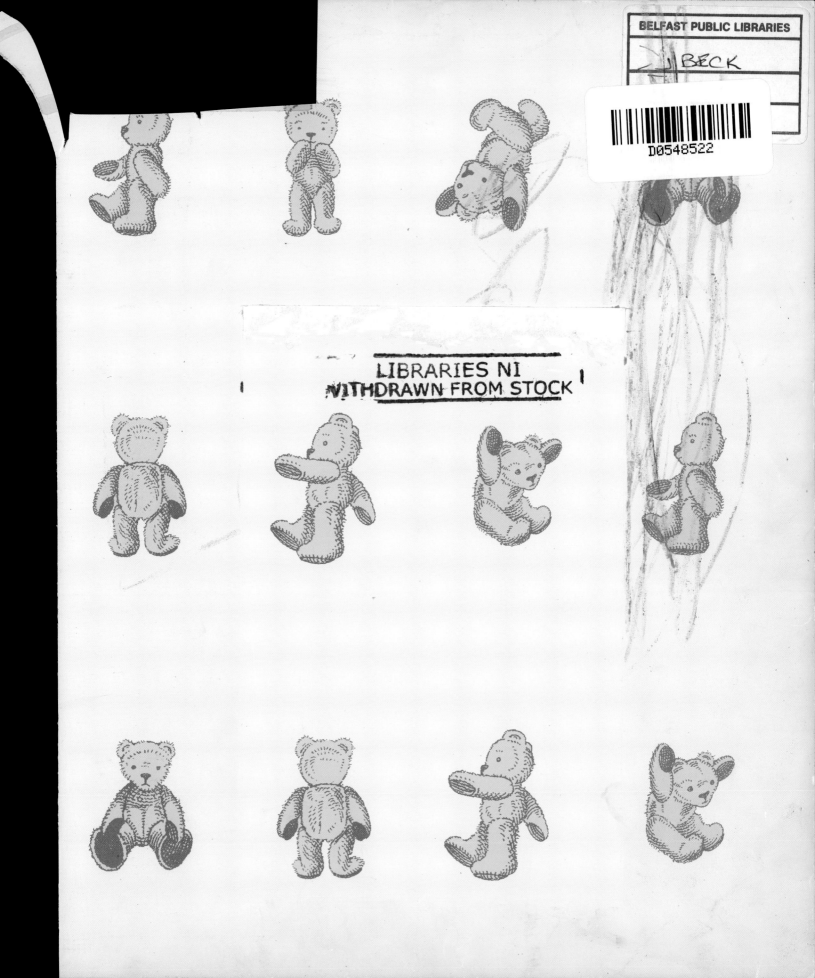

Ian Beck's
LOST
in the
SNOW

SCHOLASTIC
PRESS

For Lily.

Teddy Bears have such a quiet life,
don't they?

Scholastic Children's Books,
Commonwealth House, 1-19 New Oxford Street,
London WC1A 1NU, UK
a division of Scholastic Ltd
London ~ New York ~ Toronto ~ Sydney ~ Auckland

Published by Scholastic Ltd, 1998

Text and illustrations copyright © Ian Beck, 1998

ISBN: 0 590 54348 2 (Hardback) 0 590 11396 8 (Paperback)

Printed in Hong Kong.   All rights reserved

2 4 6 8 10 9 7 5 3 1

After a night of snow, the world was white.
Lily and Teddy looked through the window.
"We must go out and play."

"Wrap up nice and warm," said Mum. "But we'd better leave Teddy here, we don't want him to get lost."

"Poor Teddy." Lily wrapped him in a scarf, and put him on the window ledge, so that he could see the snow. "Be careful now," she said.

Before they went out, Mum banged shut the window. She didn't see Teddy sitting out there.

Whoosh! Teddy was catapulted high into the cold air.

Bump! He slid down a roof!
Boing! He bounced off an icy washing line . . .

. . . and flew on, far above the houses and trees.

Until he landed . . . plomp! . . . head first in a
snow drift.

He pulled himself up out of the snow.

Teddy took a deep breath in the wonderful crisp air. He began to explore but his paws slipped on a plank of wood.

He lost his balance and whoops! He was sliding
fast down the steep hill!

He was snowboarding. It was such
fun that he tried it over and over again.

Until he ended upside down against a tree in a field of fresh snow.

He stomped round and round, up and down, making lots of deep crunchy pawprints.

Then he decided to make a big snow bear and, when he had finished, he gave it his own warm scarf to wear.

He spotted an icy pond that looked just right
for sliding on. He ran at top speed and . . .

Wheeeee . . . eee . . . eee. . . ee . . .

. . . he slid right across.

And fell flat on his face in the cold snow.

When he stood up, his paws were cold. He felt lost and alone. It started to snow again.

The frosty wind blew up and it snowed harder
and harder. Teddy began to trudge home.

But he was soon lost in the snow.

After what seemed a very long time,
he heard a kindly voice. "Hop on here and
I'll take you home."

Teddy snuggled up under a warm blanket in a whizzing sleigh.

Soon Teddy was dropped safely home, back on to the window ledge. "I must go," called the voice. "I have much to do . . ."

Lily brought Teddy in from the cold.
"Come on," she said, "let's get you warm."

"You missed all the fun today, Teddy," said Lily, "but now it is time for bed."

Lily hugged Teddy. "Tonight is a special
night," she whispered.

Good Night, Lily. Kiss kiss.
And Good Night, Teddy. Sleep tight.
But we know what really happened, don't we?